ALPHABEARS

By Kathleen Hague
Illustrated by Michael Hague

Methuen Children's Books
LONDON

First published in Great Britain in 1984 by Methuen Children's Books Ltd.
11 New Fetter Lane, London EC4P 4EE,
by arrangement with Holt, Rinehart and Winston of New York.

ISBN: 0-416-50180-X

Printed in the United States of America

Composition: Waldman Graphics, Inc., Pennsauken, New Jersey, USA
Color Separations: Offset Separations Corporation, Turin, Italy
Offset Printing and Binding: Krueger, New Berlin, Wisconsin, USA

Designer: Marc Cheshire

To Devon, who's just like his Pop. —K.H.
To my old teddy bear, Potts. —M.H.

A is for Amanda, a good teddy bear
A barrow of apples she wheels everywhere.

B is for Byron, who snuggles in bed
Mum tucks him in with a kiss on the head.

C is for Charles, a stuffy old bear

He wears a bow tie and he brushes his hair.

D is for Devon, who's just like his pop

Their noses are big and their ears sort of flop.

E is for Elsie, an explorer bear

She went to the jungle because it was there.

F is for Freddie, a quite frightful mess

What Freddie's been up to no one can guess.

G is for Gilbert, a gruff grizzly bear

Whenever he growls you'd better beware.

H is for Henry, who loves hot pancakes

With honey and butter like Mum always makes.

I is for Ivan, an itchy brown bear

He loves to be scratched—first here, then there.

J is for John, who loves jam and jelly

It's easy to see, just look at his belly.

K is for Kyle, a kite-flying bear

He loves days that are breezy and fair.

L is for Laura, who doesn't like lightning

She thinks that the sound of thunder is frightening.

M is for Marc, a mysterious bear

Whenever you visit, you won't find him there.

N is for Nikki—that's just her nickname

Her real name is Ninny, her mother's to blame.

O is for Oliver, a one-year-old bear

He's just learned to walk, but can't climb a stair.

P is for Pam, who loves a parade

She also likes popcorn and pink lemonade.

Q is for Quimbly, a soft quilted bear

Who was sewn by hand with much love and care.

R is for Robert, who thinks that it's great

To sit by the fire and read until late.

S is for Sarah, a snow-loving bear

Just give her a hat and warm mittens to wear.

T is for Tammy, who wrinkles her nose

When you tickle her tummy, her chin, or her toes.

U is for Ursula, an unusual bear

Who seems to do nothing but just sit and stare.

V is for Vera, a kind gentle vet

She lovingly takes care of anyone's pet.

W is for William, the great wonder bear

He wears a white cape and soars through the air.

X is the way that this bear marks his place

So when he returns he can find the same space.

Y is for York, who's a very young bear

To sit at the table he needs a high chair.

Z is for Zak, who says that it is true

That zippers do better than buttons can do.

From Amanda to Zak, the bears are at ease

Because now they can say their A, B, Cs.